THE BROWN DIARY

SNEHA SARMAH

INDIA · SINGAPORE · MALAYSIA

ISBN
Paperback 979-8-89632-841-4
Hardcase 979-8-89673-759-9

CONTENTS

Contents

Prologue ... 7

Chapter One ... 11

Chapter Two ... 14

Chapter Three ... 17

Chapter Four ... 20

Chapter Five ... 24

Chapter Six ... 27

Chapter Seven ... 30

Chapter Eight ... 33

Chapter Nine ... 38

Prologue Continued ... 42

Chapter Ten ... 46

Chapter Eleven ... 51

Chapter Twelve ... 56

Chapter Thirteen ... 59

Chapter Fourteen ... 63

Chapter Fifteen ... 68

Those who love and lose,
often drown in their own tears.

PROLOGUE

"**M**ama let be swing by myself," a little girl said, as I walked inside the Vol's Park searching for an empty bench.

It is almost time for the sun to set. I scanned around but he was nowhere to be found. In a distance, I saw a bench so I walked up to it and sat in one corner, pressing my cheek against my hand placed on the bench's arm.

"The dusky sky is so captivating" Arren said while sitting down on the other side of the bench.

"Hi, how are you doing?" he said.

"Not good." I replied with a straight face.

"I know I can feel you; it hurts me the same," Arren said and placed his head on the upper back rail of the bench.

"No, it doesn't; I don't want your sympathy. For God's sake don't pretend. People don't miss someone they keep no contact with" I said.

"This used to be her favourite place to hang out with me," Arren exclaimed ignoring me.

"Just stop it, why would you act like that you miss her?" I spoke.

"I'm just saying a fact!" he exclaimed and continued "By the way, what's the matter? Why did you call me here?"

"I want you to be serious about it and realise the whole scene. It's something that I feel is important to show you," I said in a shaky voice.

With trembling hands, I took out a diary from my bag and extended it towards him and kept it on his lap. My sweaty palms almost left an impression of two thumbs on each vertical edge of the diary's leather hardcover.

"Whose diary is it; I mean why are you giving me this for?" Arren said in a stunned voice.

"You'll get all the answers to your questions if you dare to read this diary."

"I really want you to read this for once please, just for once- I pleaded and asked him to go through it thoroughly"

"Okay, but you look anxious. Are you alright?" he asked.

"Yes" I replied.

"I guess you should go through it. Can you? Please!"

He slowly turned over the hard cover and read the quote written in cursive on the very first page of it-

"This's the story of my life,

Here's the real me,

It's about the part that nobody ever heard

and the reason I kept it here so well concealed

is because I never wanted to be judged."

He gave me a look of confusion mixed with fear and continued to read the lines written between parentheses at the very bottom of the page.

"Wish I could confront it to the person concerned and not write it all just to keep it to myself…"

Arren gave me the same stare again and looked back to the diary.

CHAPTER ONE

Last Thursday of June 2022, sharp 9 A.M, I opened the website that read- Shyla Shay, has qualified the HSC with 364 marks out of 500. My heart palpitations increased as I told my result to my mother. To my surprise, she didn't react much and she wasn't sad about it either but, my soul sank when I realised that I was no longer the studious girl who never settled for average marks. The "average" that was defined by my parents, the average that was really not an average but like getting a second position in a competition which isn't really talked about much.

The whole day was a chaos. People came to ask and congratulate about it but, I knew that it wasn't a satisfactory result. By the time the sun set my tutor and my father was busy discussing about what to do further, where to study and what to study. The 24 hours felt like a whole month. Every single minute was very crucial. Finally, the clock hits 11 P.M. and it was time to sleep. My father barely kissed my forehead and wished me good night, I walked straight to my room and asked Aiden to lock the door. As soon as he locked, tears started to roll down my cheeks which I somehow managed to hold back since morning. Aiden came near to console me and said, "You did your best and deep inside everybody is happy for your outcome." And continued saying that he is privileged to have an older sibling like me...I knew he was doing all that to cheer me up but it had no effect on me since my results did not match my own expectations.

Shortly he slept after an intense conversation on the further scopes of subjects to study and I sat at the extreme corner of the bed pondering how drastically my life has changed in the last few years and where did everything go wrong. The midnight overthinking hits as usual. So, after investing hours on my thoughts, I decided what would it be and how I would line up my life ahead- a mere idea of it. The clock hit 3 A.M. and I realised it's too early to wake up! So, I finally went to sleep.

CHAPTER TWO

It was August and suddenly life was worth living again! Somehow this month gives me so much hope to restart everything I left unfinished and relive moments that seems so ordinary.

As I was inhaling the goodness of the month, a message pops up saying- "let's catch up" and my face was decorated with a silly grin. It was from my boyfriend, Arren Blake. Instantly I opened the chat box and replied to his text with a "sure" and a red heart emoji. I was all excited to see him though we live in the same city but it's a different feeling when you get to see your boyfriend, you know!

Aiden walked inside my room while I was giggling looking at the phone so he asked me, "Today's your first love anniversary, isn't it?" I nodded my head, grinning. He remembered it because few days earlier he saw the brand-new watch I bought for him and it was then when he asked me for whom was it for and I said for Arren to gift him on our anniversary.

I opened my wardrobe and picked out a nice dress, decked up for the date and left as he was waiting down the street near my home.

I saw a tall man waving at me continuously as I was heading down the street. Few steps more and my eyebrows raised in awe when I saw Arren- his shirt was in shades of Autumn, black trousers, dark brown shoes and his hair rocking in the breeze. As I came closer to him, he hugged me tight, kissed my forehead and gave me bouquet of red roses. After that we went to the cafe we often visit and then to our favourite place-Vol's Park to spend the evening where he promised me that I can count on him forever and we would be together all along. Kissing my forehead again and another on my lips he dropped me near my house. It was a pleasant day with my love. This man has no idea how happy he makes me. His existence is a blessing.

I guess August's special for me only because he exists in my life. The forbidden thought strikes my mind that what if I have to live a life without him? My mind could make my day worst with all the questions that lingers inside it. I have no idea of that "what if?" but I know it crystal clear that I don't want to live that life where he doesn't exist.

A year back August gave me the most adored, treasured, the once in a lifetime kind of person. I reckon how could life offer me something I never knew I wanted until I had it. It was then when I realised this is going to be my everything and losing it would take away my everything.

CHAPTER THREE

Shyla Shay- the professor uttered aloud. "One more year to go before you graduate from this institution and you have a lot to improve. You can expand your knowledge if you care to spend some time digging the books in the library. This university has so much to offer but these brats won't care until it's too late."

He started to lecture us. The whole classroom echoed with his words. I never thought that sitting in a big classroom would be so annoying rather it would be easier to escape from the cranky professors.

An hour later he left the classroom and went to his cabin. I know, he would sit with his leg one above the other and place it on top of the table, munching snacks that Ma'am Sia brings for him every day. I wonder why does his wife not prepare anything for him, nobody would want a radio that start playing something you are least interested to hear that too early in the morning.

All the students started to vent about the forbidden radio, Ma'am Sia's favourite, Jos Harvey who looks no less than a frustrated lobby attendant; specs always on the tip of his nose somehow managing to defy gravity.

"The only lecture he manages to give is after the results are declared. His whole session would pass just by sitting in his cabin munching Ma'am Sia's handmade snacks." One spoke.

The other went on by saying, "how can we manage the whole syllabus by ourself, we need a teacher who would care to clear our doubts and do the lessons on time."

I agreed to nearly everyone. I didn't take a chance by disagreeing.

Everybody started to pack their bags and left frustrated while I sat in the classroom for a while wondering what would my parents react to my average marks though they don't say much nowadays but the silent disappointment their faces reflect is something I hate the most.

CHAPTER FOUR

It's been a year and nothing really changed, but now when I take a glance back to those days everything seems so different. Nobody really cares about my existence; I merely excite people and they hardly try to understand how depressing it is to be "ME". "Come have your dinner" my mom called. With no appetite I walked out of my room and joined them at the dining table.

Arren and I had a fight over something silly and he hasn't texted me since last evening. It was half past midnight; I tried to call him but he didn't answer so I called him again and again in hope that he might pick one. All of the calls were unanswered, I kept staring at my phone continuously checking if there's a text or call from him and shortly a message popped up on my phone- "I'm at Jolly's place for a slumber" along with a video.

The video was about everybody dancing and having drinks and most importantly- Jolly sitting right next to him smiling at the camera with the broadest smile of all times while he was filming it. I could feel my heart palpitations on my tongue. My hands started to shiver. Something about the video wasn't right, I can sense it. I questioned myself, "Why over Jolly's place?"

My eyes squinted with a frown at this thought. It wasn't something that happened before.

He hated slumbers. He didn't join his best friend's slumber party and faked a severe headache to escape it earlier.

But this question kept lingering inside my head that why did he agree at Jolly's place? I couldn't sleep, rolling left and right in the bed thinking what could be the reason to join her slumber party.

Next morning I texted him- "Meet me at the garden down the Parker's Street"

"At a time that suits you"

He replied within a minute- "Not today, I want to rest a bit, my body aches from last night, will catch you soon."

I called him immediately but it beeped twice and announced that it was switched off. Something was fishy...

*****

The sun glazing with yellowish-orange light was always an amusing event to watch from my room's window. I like my room like no other place. The comfort and relaxation it provides me with, ahh! It the only place where I can be myself.

The sky turned red and the sun was hardly visible. My eyes were fixated on the view from my window.

"Guess who forgot about her best friend?" someone exclaimed in a sweet voice. It was Pollie, the most joyous person in my life. Someone I've known since kindergarten. Suddenly all my worries vanished as we started to gossip about our lives, how she's doing and stuffs. My mom entered holding a tray full of snacks that were Pollie's favourite. She loved Pollie. Shortly she left closing the door.

All of a sudden, I noticed a concerned look on Pollie's face. It made me edgy and so I asked her, "What's the matter? Are you alright?"

"I'm all fine nothing to worry about!" she exclaimed.

"How are you doing? Why did you not contact me after all these and suffered all alone all along?" Pollie sputtered.

CHAPTER FIVE

DATED 6 SEPTEMBER, 2023

I believe that "being the villain is so much better than being the victim." And guess what," I am a victim, a victim of love."

"It twitches my soul to learn that I was never loved by the people who I thought, loved me the most."

"I was blessed with a person whom I made my comfort zone and that's when he turned into a curse."

I miss him so much, but the worst part is that he is no longer mine. He doesn't miss me as much as I do! Probably forgot about my existence.

There comes a thought that runs down my veins interpreting as- "you'll miss him forever." But what am I going to miss?

"The I love you(s) he never said, the assurance he never gave or the love we never made?"

It wasn't all true but it wasn't false either. There's a series of feelings crossing my mind, all analysed raw.

"For once I want to love without any fears or tears."

I've cried my heart out for nearly every night since he left. I couldn't accept the fact that everything changed in a snap of a finger. The love, the promises and everything we dreamt together.

"The human greed to crave for things we don't have is malignant."

I never thought that Arren would ever cheat on me. Everything was so fine and reckless in our relationship until one random night he chose to sleep with another girl.

How can people change so quickly? Aren't they haunted by their past actions? Do they not think how much the other person have to suffer? How heartless one could be?

I sighed! I knew I had no answer to those questions neither do I have him to answer my questions.

Millions of thoughts but too stunned to do anything about it.

Huh! I guess that's what my life's about, "trauma, tragedy and tears."

CHAPTER SIX

The children that were playing in the playground since afternoon were returning home as it was getting dark. They looked so happy and were enjoying by making snowballs and throwing them at their friends while they walked down the road. This scene always reminds me that it's time for Christmas. I closed my window and sat near the fireplace sipping my coffee.

"It's freezing outside" Aiden said as he walked in carrying a box of pastries.

I sipped my evening coffee and devoured the flavourful pastry.

"what's special about this year's Christmas?" Aiden asked.

It quickly triggered my flashback memory, when Arren used to ask me the same question when we used to meet for an evening coffee and sat down in the cafe discussing everything about the Christmas plans for our families.

"What are you thinking about? I asked what's special about this Christmas?" he said aloud.

I couldn't think of anything at that moment so I said, "Just wait, it would definitely be special. I'll plan it with Pollie, she would surely like the idea." He gave a thumbs-up and left.

But I wasn't sure whether Pollie would join us to celebrate Christmas together or not, since I gave hopes to Aiden, I freaked out and called her to confirm about her plans for Christmas.

"Hello Pollie, how have you been?" I said as she answered my call.

"Just good, what about you?" she asked in more of a concerned voice.

"What are your plans for Christmas? Have you decided something yet?" I went straight to the point before she could ever ask me about Arren.

She said, "no, I haven't planned anything yet." It was a relief for me so I asked her whether she would mind planning it out together this time. We talked for almost an hour planning for the Christmas and she sounded so happy about the idea of celebrating Christmas together. Everything started to feel quite good but at the same time the flashbacks kept piercing my heart.

At night as we sat to dine, I announced about the Christmas plans for the year. Everybody agreed and looked happy about it.

CHAPTER SEVEN

"**I** drowned in the same eyes I've fallen for."

I couldn't hold back my tears anymore.

I miss him so much, literally every single day!!! I can never get over this. Oh God! What have you done to me. I can't stop thinking about it- the sunsets, the weekends, the…wait I don't get it, how is it so easy for him to not think about what we had back together and act like he never loved me?

Not again, these questions inside my head will make me insane someday.

But how do I not think of him, I love him so much!

I remember how earnest his promises were that he made on our first anniversary. His enthusiasm wasn't fake. The way he took my hand and kissed it, making an eye contact wasn't fake.

The way he grabbed my waist and kissed me so passionately making sure that there isn't any part of me unassured, felt so divine. It was definitely not fake, I believe.

He tucked my hair behind my ears and whispered "I love you sweetheart; you have no idea how much you mean to me." I closed my eyes and slightly tilted my head to feel his lips on mine.

Everything felt so real that day. Reminiscing about that day made me miss him so much more. I couldn't contain my emotions to myself, I wanted to talk to him. I haven't heard his voice since so long. I decided to call him so I picked my phone and searched for "Love bug" in my contacts.

I stared at the number for a moment while my mind played a flashback of why he isn't mine anymore. It humbled me instantly.

I sighed and kept my phone on the table realising I made a good decision by not dialling his number.

CHAPTER EIGHT

"What do you mean?" I asked.

"I know you're good at supressing your emotions in front of people, but you can't lie to me," Pollie said confidently.

"I don't know what are you talking about!"

"What emotions? Be clear Pollie," I said.

"You and Arren!" she exclaimed with a scowl.

"Arren? What did he say to you?"

"We didn't talk," she said.

"Then? What is it about? Tell me Pollie, I'm curious." I said inquisitively.

"Today, I went on a brunch with my boyfriend down the Coal streets. While having our food I accidently spilled the soup on my dress so I went to the restroom to clean my dress where I saw Arren kissing a girl."

"She is your professor's daughter, Mr. Jos Harvey, whom lives next to my house. Um Jolly, you know her I guess…the girl who showed up with Mr. Harvey at my parents' anniversary last year."

"Moreover, I've noticed that lately Arren has been visiting her place frequently. I didn't know that y'all broke up neither did you call me up to talk about it or anything."

"I thought they're good friends until today, when I saw them together doing those stuffs."

"I'm sorry, I just wanted to check on you." Pollie narrated the whole drama, the drama I was unaware of.

I was flabbergasted, my soul shattered into a million pieces. I was in complete disbelief. My throat dried out and tears rolled down my cheeks.

Pollie saw me wiping my tears with shaky hands. She might be thinking that I'm crying over my break up but she had no idea that she's the one who unveiled everything happening behind my back. It was only now when I knew that he is now Jolly's 'love bug' not mine."

"It's only now that I know we broke up." I quavered.

"What do you mean Shyla?" she said.

"He kept this under the hat for so long. The fact that he was over me and was deliberately cheating on me with that moll Jolly!"

"Yesternight, he attended Jolly's slumber party, which seemed so odd as he never really enjoyed slumbers. Today morning I texted Arren asking him to meet me, but he said his body aches from last night and wanted to rest."

"I wonder why his body aches! Bloody scumbag, he was making out with that cunt and I was freaking the fuck out of me because I couldn't figure out why was he acting so weird lately."

I uttered and grimaced.

My sadness turned into disgust and anger. My body went through a rollercoaster of emotions.

I don't know what's worse- "Arren making out and fucking my professor's daughter or the fact that I got cheated by a guy who acted so in love with me."

"I-I'm sorry Shyla! I'm shocked. I don't really understand how could he do this." Pollie said in disbelief.

"Cut the crap, let it me. You can't change someone who doesn't see a fault in their actions, you know!" I said.

My mind still couldn't process what just happened, but I didn't want to wail in front of Pollie so I put up a facade until she left.

*****

It was ten past eight when Pollie left.

I locked myself in the room and sat on the floor. I stared at the wall for few minutes questioning my life.

I was in denialism. I wasn't ready to accept the fact the Arren cheated on me. How could he manage to deceive me into believing that he loved me while he fucking didn't.

Everything was a pretend. Everything we had was fake, neither the love nor the promises he made.

Promises aren't made to be broken. People need to understand that because some people live by them.

I grieved over the backstabbing and disloyalty for the entire night, wishing that it wasn't real or just a nightmare that I could erase from my memory.

Aiden sat on the floor for an hour trying to convince me to have dinner but all I could do was just sob and sob and sob. I requested him to tell mom that I've slept because of my headache.

It's a day that haunts me every time I think about it.

It made me hate the month of August. I unloved August- the month that made me feel so in love, but how do I unlove him? Even though I hate him for whatever he has done I can never unlove him. He was so well entangled in my heart...

I didn't deserve any of it at all. The betrayal, the tears or the abandon.

CHAPTER NINE

It's Christmas eve's morning. Suddenly the doorbell rang and my mom went to open the door. It was Pollie with her mom and dad.

"Welcome! Mr. and Mrs. Roxy, how have y'all been?" my mom said. Uncle and aunty greeted them as well.

Pollie hugged my mother and said "good morning aunty!"

My mom sweetly smiled and wished her.

Our parents sat together and had breakfast meanwhile Pollie and I wanted to buy some presents and confectioneries for Christmas.

"May I join y'all?" Aiden said.

"Why not," Pollie replied.

So, all three of us headed down the street. The weather was so cold outside that we hurried up with whatever stuffs we had to buy and planned on returning as soon as possible.

On the way while returning home, Pollie asked "What are you thinking about? you look so lost. Is everything fine?"

She looked at Aiden with confusion. They had no idea of what was going inside my head. They didn't bother me at first and we continued to walk our way home with more discussions for Christmas.

When we got home, Pollie was shivering and was really cold. My mom noticed her and said, "Come here Pollie, sit here near the fireplace."

"Hurry up, we have so much to plan for tonight and we are short of time." She said excitedly and walked away to sit near the fireplace.

*****

Everybody had their dinner and went to bed. My mom was doing the dishes alone so I went to help her.

"Let me help you mom, you've been working all day," I said.

"No baby, it's alright," she sweetly said and smiled.

But I made her wash her hands and asked her to sit on the chair aside while I did all the remaining dishes. I was done doing. I washed my hands and wiped my hands on my mom's clothes. I kissed her on both the cheeks, her forehead and both her hands. My eyes were filled with tears. She saw my face and said, "What happened my dear? Why are you crying?" she held up my face with her hands placed on my cheeks.

"I love you mom; I love you so much! I just wanted to say this before the year ends nothing else mom, good night." I said and kissed her forehead again.

*****

"I don't know what I was doing before you because you've been so important to me ever since we met. But the fact that I've to stand an 'after you' lends me no clue of what to do."

I tried; I swear I tried until I couldn't.

You know, "The greatest scandal to ever happen is with the ones who drown in their own tears."

It was all. Yes, the end. The end to the questions. The questions that linger inside my head.

PROLOGUE
CONTINUED

Arren's blood ran cold, I could tell from his face. He was in dismay and kept staring that page of the diary on his lap awe-stricken. He was definitely knocked for six after reading the diary.

After a minute I chose to break the silence and said "So?" before I could complete my sentence he flinched and looked at me.

His eyes were brimmed with tears and a drop dripped down on the page.

"I-I really, h-how could, w-what," he stuttered and barely said something that could make some sense.

Though he was tongue-tied but the guilt on his face was clearly visible. He started sweating and unbuttoned the collar of his shirt and adjusted his sweater so that air could pass by. Slowly his body gestured nervousness and remorse.

He looked around with his teary eyes; clutching the arm beside him. I opine he got flashbacks of the times when he and Shyla visited the place because he said it was their favourite place to be.

He still didn't utter a single word and was lost in his guilt filled thoughts.

"It didn't have to be this way, you know! It was all your fault; you knew her very well Arren. She was so sure about you, but you ditched her. You didn't even care to contact her later, check on her that how she's been or apologise for the stupid drama you played with her."

"Why did you cheat on her? Just why? I don't understand the point of cheating on a girl who was so down on her knees for you." In a quavering voice, I railed.

"I-It was just a fling for me, I didn't realise that she loved me immensely and that my existence in her life would create a huge difference so much so that she wouldn't take her alone live into consideration if I wasn't in it."

"I took her to be one of those girls who have a very fragile heart, over-sensitive and easily triggered my one's actions." Arren said as if this could undo everything that had happened.

"But she could've called me or text me or could've simply showed up to my place. We could've talked about it." He added.

"Talked about what? The cheating? Oh, sorry the fling, right?"

"For once let's forget about what you did, couldn't you do the same what you expected from her? Especially when it was all your fault." I said throatily.

He stood up holding the diary close to his chest. Abruptly I heard him sobbing, the diary still close to his chest as if he was hugging Shyla. I got misty-eyed; I didn't know how to react to that situation and so kept staring at him.

After a while, I heard a feeble voice saying "It's always too late to love back people who loved you."

"The last stage of loving someone is to mourn for them. I see, it cost her own life just because she loved me. I know I'm the reason for everything she did to herself."

"Yeah, you're correct. Too late; you can't reverse it back to how it was."

"She drowned in her own tears; the tears she shed for you."

"You should've treasured her when she was yours because nothing can be possessed forever." I said lamenting.

Looking at the diary he said "Please let me keep this with me, please Pollie, I plead you!"

"NO!" I shouted at him as I didn't want to give it at first but he kept sobbing and pleading so I agreed and said "Fine, keep it but I hope you don't lose it."

"Never!" he said and kissed the brown hardcover of the diary.

CHAPTER
TEN

" Shyla and I were sitting near the fireplace; discussing about the plans for Christmas eve. I started stating my ideas about the night, but Shyla was lost to the world. She barely paid attention to what I said. She looked sad and terrified so I asked her, "Shyla! What are you thinking about? You look so lost."

She flinched at my voice and said "well, nothing like that!"

"I know you're lying. Come on, tell me what's disturbing you?"

"Even when we were out to buy presents you looked lost in your thoughts. Tell me please." I compelled her.

"Nothing new Pollie, you know what makes me feel so uneasy." She said.

"You're thinking about him, right?" I spoke.

She nodded looking down.

"It something you can't change Shyla. I guess you should stop thinking about it and move on, I know it's hard to forget someone you've loved but you have to" I said.

"But I can't Pollie; I just can't. how am I supposed to forget someone I love so thirstily, someone I counted on for everything…"

"I tried to not think about what happened between us but the voices inside my head, the questions he left unanswered haunts me so much. Life's so unfair at times, the ardent lovers suffer the most." She said with contempt.

"The world would've been different if everybody followed the morals of life, but it isn't so…

Now or later, he will be guilty for his actions." I uttered.

"What if latter's too late?" Shyla said inquisitively.

I swerved my chair towards her that was placed facing the fireplace.

"What does that mean?" I asked her.

She didn't answer rather gave me a stare that screamed hopelessness. I could sense her distressing thoughts through her words.

We sat in silence until Aiden came and asked us "So, what have you'll discussed?" in a cherry voice.

Shyla suddenly stood up and left without uttering a word as if she was frustrated. Aiden and I looked at each other in confusion; having no clue about her behaviour. After a while he said, "What happened to her?"

"She didn't say anything clearly, but it's about Arren and something she didn't mention. I know, she's cooking some sort of matter inside her head which she doesn't want to talk about." I said Aiden.

*****

The evening, we had a celebration at Shyla's place. Aiden helped me with the decorations while my mom and aunt Rebecca made the bouffe for the party. Shyla was in her room all alone watching the dark sky through her window. I went to see what was she doing because she didn't show up even for once since the evening.

Before I could ask her, aunt Rebecca came inside the room and said "Where have you been Shyla? Why are you sitting in your room?"

"Nothing just a mild headache mom, I'm going to pack the gifts." She said and left with a plastic smile on her face.

I followed her and said from behind "Why did you lie to your mom? You're acting so strange since a long time now, tell me what the fuck has happened? What are you up to?"

She said in a feeble voice "I was reminiscing my last Christmas with Arren. Everything around here reminds me of him. The times were so good, now when I look back it seems surreal. How crazy those days were. I wish he were mine, Pollie."

"Stop thinking about him and enjoy the Christmas!" I said almost losing my mind.

"I wish I could, but I can't." she said and left with the presents and wrapping papers.

CHAPTER
ELEVEN

Everybody was tired after the celebration and almost everyone was in their rooms except for aunt Rebecca; she was doing the dishes. I asked her whether she needed any help but she denied and told me to sleep instead.

I wished her good night and as I turned, she said "Don't forget to set an alarm for tomorrow! The prayer starts sharp 9 in the morning we need to be there on time. And yes, please remind Shyla as well."

I nodded and walked to Shyla's room. As I entered her room, I saw her writing something in a book which looked similar to a tome.

"You haven't slept yet?" she asked with yet another plastic smile on her face as if I didn't notice her hide the book under the pillow but I pretended like I didn't see her do it.

"Where is Aiden?" I asked.

"He went to his friend's place for the eve's party. he'll be back early morning," she said.

"Oh, I forgot to say that Aunt Rebecca said to set an alarm because we need to be at the church before 9 A.M. tomorrow."

"Good night" I said and walked out of the room wondering why did she hide the book. It's even more strange because she didn't ask me to sit down for a gossip session or sleep in her room because she doesn't like sleeping alone.

Lately her actions were awfully strange and she gave me literally no clue about whatever she was thinking except for Arren.

The next morning was a dreadful Christmas morning.

As soon as my alarm went off, I hit the snooze button for an extra five minutes of sleep, but the five minutes was an hour ago before I could be fully awake.

It was 8 o'clock already, I freaked and sprang out of the bed. As I approached to open the door, I heard someone's shrill screech from the back corners of the house. I opened the door and ran towards Shyla's room to see who was it.

I slowed my pace at a distance when I saw aunt Rebecca sitting on the floor with her back against the door of Shyla's room and her head tilted to the left looking up. It was terrifying to see her sit like that with no emotions on her face. I approached her with steady steps and when I reached the door and took a glance at what she was staring up at Shyla's room my blood ran cold. My hands and legs were stiffed and I could barely believe the scene I just witnessed.

My mom shrieked with ache; my dad gasped with his eyes wide open standing right beside my mom trying to believe what they just saw. I looked around wondering how to handle aunt Rebecca, she sat there like a soulless body. It was an incredulous situation- "scary enough to be a reality and too late to be nightmare."

I sat on my haunches and with my shaky hands I held aunt Rebecca's shoulders trying to fight my fears and speak something but I didn't know what to say. Her vision was fixated up.

I turned my head forcing my eyeballs to see towards the dangling feet, the drooped face hanging from the thick white rope and the body with stiff hands and legs hang down. That's my best friend? My mind clicked; I still couldn't believe the body hanging down the fan was Shyla.

Her face screamed silence. Nothing felt real at that moment. Everybody stood frozen. With tears in my eyes and little strength I went to the room, picked up my phone to call Aiden.

"Hear me up, get home as fast as possible." I said as soon as he picked up my call.

The thought of how uncle would react to his daughter's lifeless body was beyond imagination so I waited until Aiden arrived.

After a couple of minutes, I saw Aiden come on his bike and parked it at a distance and hurried towards the gate.

"Uncle Kaz is at the garden, bring him along with you," I shouted from the balcony.

I waited at the door until they climbed up the stairs.

"What happened why did you call me in such a hurried tone? Is everything alright?" Aiden asked.

"What's the matter Pollie?" uncle Kaz uttered in a nervous note.

I looked at their faces, but I could hardly gather my guts to speak the truth. I continued looking at their faces in a pendular motion and after much hesitation I gulped my tears and said, "Shyla h-h-hanged hersel-" even before I could finish my sentence Aiden ran towards Shyla's room and uncle Kaz followed Aiden with giant strides.

CHAPTER TWELVE

2023's Christmas haunts me every single day. It was a dreadful Christmas that none would want to remember, but it's something one couldn't forget or erase from their memory either.

It been six months since the tragedy happened but the thought of it revives the pain just as it starts bleeding if one removes the eschar from their wound.

The loss of their daughter has impacted their lives so much that they haven't been the same since that day, especially Aiden because Shyla was the person he counted on for everything, their shared a bond just like best friends do. From teaching school lessons to life lessons- Shyla did it all.

I miss her every day. No one could ever take the place of a friend who has been with you since kindergarten, someone who has seen you in every phase of your life, someone who knows all of your secrets.

The loss of the Shay's family is inconceivable. No lapse of time can ever fill the void Shyla has left behind. Every time I visit her house to check on aunt and uncle, they burst out crying and only thing they ask is what could be the reason behind her ludicrous action.

Wish I could tell them how she managed to hide all her emotions from them ever since she became a teen until one day she couldn't anymore and ended up her life.

The most disturbing fact is that she didn't even trust me to discuss whatever she was going through nor even Aiden. I guess the break up left her devastated and she couldn't help herself anymore. Someone's inconsequential step can make a huge difference in another person's life.

Life's an illusion, here everyone has different facades to hide what they actually are in their true persona. Shyla was broken inside and I couldn't even help her out.

No matter how much Arren regrets his infidelity, it wouldn't bring back Shyla and so's the irony of life- "We endure tremendous pain just to learn what love isn't and that it takes a deceased body to experience what love is."

CHAPTER THIRTEEN

I followed uncle Kaz to the room.

"What happened mom?" Aiden yelled as he ran towards her.

He stopped at the door of Shyla's room with both his hands on the casing of the door either side. My mom and dad where inside the room standing next to aunt Rebecca who hasn't moved an inch from her earlier position.

I placed my hand on Aiden back and when he turned around, I saw both his cheeks were divided by a shiny line and his eyes reflected intense grieve.

Uncle Kaz sat down near aunt Rebecca and before he could speak anything about the hanging body she abruptly started crying.

"This can't be our daughter Rebecca…"

"How could she take away her life like this?" Uncle Kaz cried out.

Aunt Rebecca kept bawling. Aiden stood at the door sobbing while his eyes were fixed at the lifeless body of his sister.

All the tears and wailing from the room that day shudders my soul with terror. The tragic event changed my thoughts on how the very ordinary thing we hear about can actually haunt us forever.

*****

Uncle Kaz asked Aiden to unknot the rope and take her body to the hall. He then informed the cops.

While everyone was in the hall waiting for the cops to arrive, I went to Shyla's room.

As I walked near the bed, I saw something sticking out from underneath the pillow. I lifted the pillow; it was the diary she was writing in when I walked inside her room last night.

The brown, leather hardcover diary; similar to a tome. I picked it up and thought to keep it with me. I didn't want her family to discover about it. As I turned around, I saw Aiden standing behind me.

"You scared me!" I said but he was looking at the diary I was holding.

"I've seen Shyla writing on this for years now. She never allowed me to read it." He said and paused.

"Are you planning to take this with you?" he continued.

"Yes!"

"Please let me keep this before your parents read her diary. The reason is obvious why she wrote all these instead of speaking out to her parents. Can I?" I nearly begged before he could even answer.

"Ok fine" he said. I thanked him and walked straight up to the room where I kept my bag and buried it under my clothes.

CHAPTER FOURTEEN

"Shyla's no more!" I texted Arren.

"Stop acting like high school kids. We're never getting back" he replied.

"I'm serious, I texted you to attend her funeral tomorrow. You hated her but she couldn't unlove you; I hope you show up!" I responded to his reply.

He saw my text and immediately Aiden's phone rang, he was sitting beside me.

"It's Arren" he said.

"Pick up and keep it on speaker mode" I said.

He nodded and picked up the call.

"Yes?" Aiden said.

"Hey! Pollie texted me to visit your house tomorrow" Arren said.

"Yes, I asked her to text you and as she said- hope you show up." Aiden replied in a monotonous voice.

"Shyla's funeral?"

"How did that happen? I don't believe y'all" Arren said in startling tone.

"Fine" Aiden said and hung up the call. He was in complete grief about his sister's death and didn't want to talk to anybody.

Arren texted me seconds later, "But I'm not in the city, I'm at my grandma's home for the Christmas and new year!"

I saw the text and said it to Aiden, but he barely cared to respond and walked out of the room.

"I'll visit when I'll be there." Arren texted again.

I replied it with a "Ok".

*****

The funeral is over and I'm back to my house shortly after new year.

This was the first new year that I spent alone ever since I met Shyla. The worst part was that I spent the new year planning her funeral.

The breeze on the terrace was chilling, I climbed down the stairs to get another jacket. The month of January remains cold indeed but the incident has turned it into something that runs our blood cold too and would haunt us forever.

Suddenly I remembered the diary I brought with me from Shyla's room that I keep it in my drawer next to my bed. I ran to my room and locked the door. I was afraid at first to go through it but I eagerly wanted to read it as well, so I pulled out the drawer and picked up the brown coloured cover diary and sat in my bed. I stared at the cover for a minute wondering if it's a good idea to go through it or not but when I couldn't fight my curiosity, I opened it and started reading the pages.

Nearly after an hour or so, I closed the diary wondering how the very ordinary life has so much of extraordinary sufferings and that you'll never know which things and in what ways something can affect someone's life and how suffocating it turns out to be for them.

"Nobody questions you as much as you do to yourself", wish I could tell her this before. But whatever she thought and endured throughout, led her to choose this obscure path.

She was harsher on herself than anyone else could be. That's what sensitive people do to themselves- they live in a self-created guilt for not being someone others liked and eventually try to erase their existence when the burden heavies. Mostly because they are abandoned by their loved ones even if they pretend to be there for you, they have actually left you far behind from where they stand. So eventually you get tired of chasing them and when you make up your mind to no longer chase them and return to where you belong, it's only then when you realise, you're too far from the start and you are no longer dear to your adored ones. So, what would a fragile man do? Jump off the cliff? Certainly, yes. So did she.

It's not easy to unlove, undo the promises and leave for the ones who immerse entirely to love someone. Well, it's quite the opposite for the one who don't actually love. It's definitely a choice but what you choose has a great impact on the other person. Sometimes it's all they depend on. That's what my mind could resonate at the moment after reading her diary.

CHAPTER FIFTEEN

"You should go and visit Rebecca" my mom said.

"I did, day before yesterday."

"Aunt Rebecca would cry profusely every time I visit her and it breaks my heart to see her like that." I spoke.

We were talking about the incident and how it changed everything and everyone's life while looking at the empty afternoon sky in the balcony when I felt my phone vibrating in my trousers' pocket. I took it out from my pocket to see who it was.

I went inside the room, it was Aiden calling so I picked up the call and said, "hello!"

"Hi, I'm back home. When are we visiting Shyla's home?" he said in a soft pitch.

"Before we visit her house, meet in the Vol's Park today in the evening. And don't ask anything more; you'll know everything when we'll meet because I don't want to talk about it on the phone." I uttered fast and hanged the call with a "bye." I knew if I waited for him to speak, he would've asked me to disclose it over the call which I didn't want to happen.

*****

It was quite dark when I and Arren were returning home after we met at the Vol's Park.

He was walking ahead of me, graving the diary to his chest with his hands.

I don't know whether the guilt and regret were real, or fake and temporary. But any of these feelings won't bring back Shyla and the void will be felt forever. Only if he had this realisation earlier and showed this love when she was craving for it. Things would be so different if it happened at right time when she was in hopes of experiencing it. But it didn't and that's the worst.

Arren kept walking probably lost in his thoughts after reading the diary while holding it still close to his chest.

After a while he stopped and turned around me and said, "I hate myself for acting so absurd when I had it all. Even I wouldn't forgive myself for doing something so stupid but she did and I still couldn't see how much she loved me." His eyes were filled with tears as he spoke.

I curled my lips and nodded looking down.

He then turned to the right at the crossroad and walked down the lane, all alone in the dusky winter evening, without moving the diary even an inch.

I sighed and walked to the left thinking about the brown diary that veiled the brown feelings of Shyla.

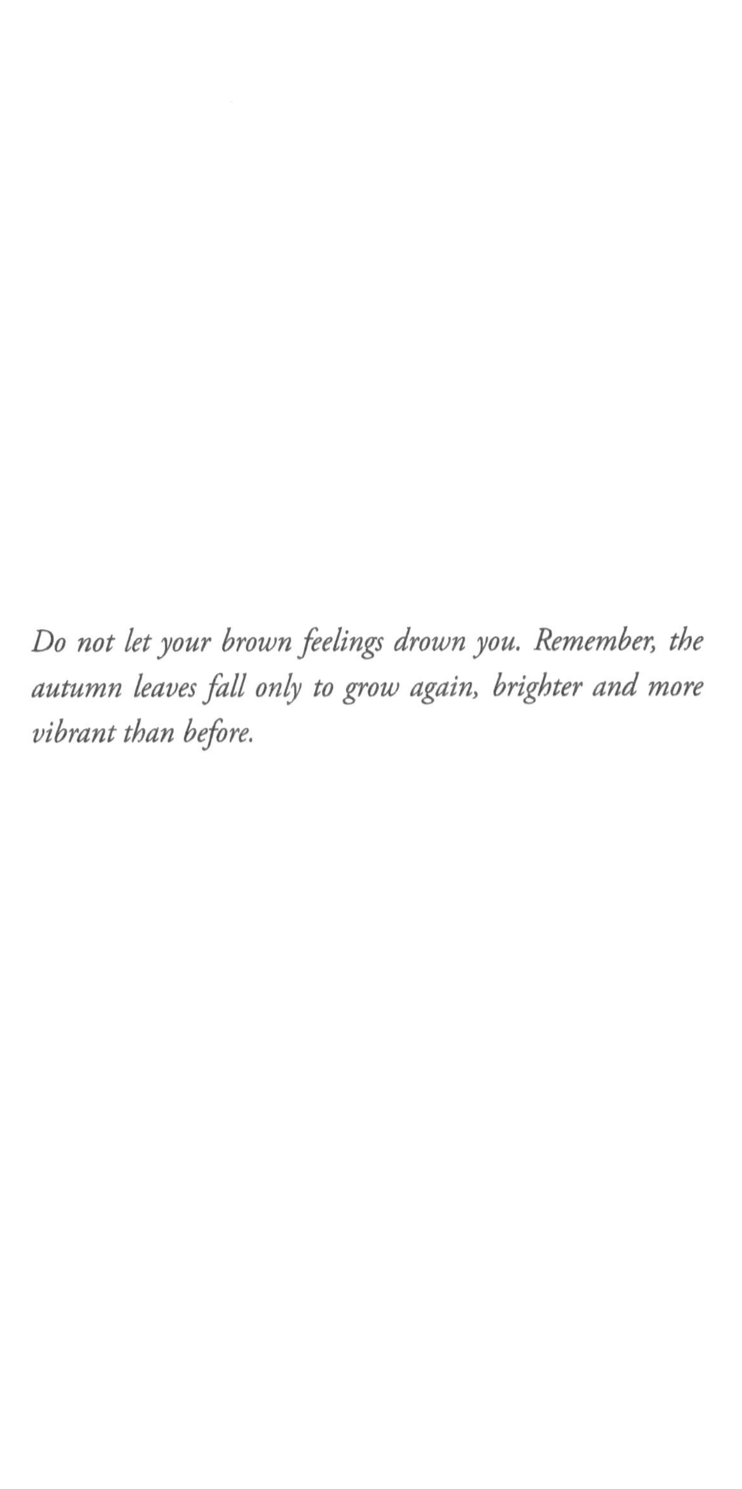

Do not let your brown feelings drown you. Remember, the autumn leaves fall only to grow again, brighter and more vibrant than before.